Mommy's Office

To Deralyn and Bethany, the best and brightest of all worlds
—B.S.H.

To Sula, Jack, Nora, and the newest member of the family, Eva,
with love, David

Printed in Hong Kong

1 2 3 4 5 6 7 8 9 10

Library of Congress Cataloging-in-Publication Data
Hazen, Barbara Shook.
  Mommy's office / by Barbara Shook Hazen; illustrated by David
Soman.—1st ed.
    p.   cm.
  Summary: Emily accompanies Mommy downtown to see where she works.
  ISBN 0-689-31601-1
  1. Mothers and daughters—Fiction. 1. Work—Fiction. I. Soman.
David, ill. II. Title.
PZ7.H314975Mo   1992
[E]—dc20   91-25013

Mommy's Office

By Barbara Shook Hazen
Illustrated by David Soman

ATHENEUM   1992   NEW YORK
Maxwell Macmillan Canada · Toronto
Maxwell Macmillan International
New York · Oxford · Singapore · Sydney

Today Mommy's taking me to her office instead of where
I go, which is sort of like my office.

I can't wait to see where Mommy works. I can't wait
to see some of the things she talks about that I don't
understand.

We go all the way downtown on the big city bus with
a lot of grown-ups. I try to act very grown-up too.

When we get off, Mommy points out the window
where she works. It's so high up that it's hard to see.

At my office, the window is on the ground and has pictures in it.

We have to take an elevator to get to Mommy's office.
Everyone pushes, which is scary. I get squished and
almost lose Mommy's hand.

I'm glad that where I go isn't up so high.

When we get out, a nice lady greets us. She shakes my hand and takes my coat and says, "I'd know you anywhere, Emily."

I don't know how she knows.

First I want to see where Mommy works.
Mommy's office has a desk and a chair, just like mine.
Her desk has piles of paper on it, just like mine
sometimes.
The best part is a big picture of me on top of the
biggest pile.
Now I know how the lady knows I'm Emily.

Mommy lets me try her twirly chair and her telephone
to call Gram and say, "Guess where I am?"

Then she shows me how to make a necklace out of paper clips.

She starts me and I finish, the way Mrs. Sethness does at my office.

Then Mommy says, "Work time. I have a presentation to give this afternoon, and I have paperwork to do."

"I do paperwork too," I say.

"I know you do," Mommy says, pointing to a piece of mine on her wall.

Mommy gives me crayons and paper and we both work
on our paperwork.

I make the most pieces.

When we're finished, Mommy takes me to a machine to copy our paperwork.

She lets me push the buttons myself. I make copies of my best pieces for Daddy and Gram and Mrs. Sethness.

Next we go to Mommy's coffee break.
It's one of the things Mommy's talked about, but it isn't
what I thought.
   Nobody breaks anything and everybody is very polite.

It's like cookies and milk at my office, only better because the doughnuts have jelly insides.

After coffee break, Mommy has a friend over. They compare paperwork and talk about the presentation.

I have rest period on Mommy's raincoat and wonder what kind of presents.

Lunch is next and is one of the nicest things about Mommy's office. I get to push a tray and pick anything I want. And everybody wants to know what I do, so I tell them.

After lunch, it's time for Mommy's presentation.
It's in a room as big as the one for our Christmas party.
But it isn't like Christmas because there aren't any
presents.

Mommy's presentation is more like show-and-tell at my office.

Mommy shows a new kind of toothpaste and tells why
it is better than any other kind ever.
I clap the most for Mommy.

Then it's time to go. I thank everyone and say
good-bye.
　I show the nice lady who gets my coat how I can put
it on myself, backwards. She says, "I could
never do that," which makes me glad I can.

Going down, I don't get squished or scared.

On the bus, Mommy asks me what I liked best about her office.

I say, "Lots of things—like lunch and my paper-clip
necklace and your twirly chair and all the nice people.
    "But very best was seeing what you do and that
we do sort of the same things."

That'll be nice to remember when I'm back at
my office.